The Talking Dolls

D1509643

By Camaryn Wheeler

ACKNOWLEDGEMENTS

First of all, I'd like to thank my publishing team for making all of this possible. I'd also like to thank my Mom, Dad, and my sister Jamison, for encouraging me to complete my book. The character Casity is actually inspired by my sister. Thanks, JJ! Love you!

I'd also like to thank my friends, especially, my best friend Johanna. You kept me going while I was writing it in third and fourth grade.

Thanks to all my family and teachers, including Mrs. Steinmetz, who helped to keep it a secret until the book was finally published.

I'd also like to thank my Grandmothers who suffered through the times when I forced them to listen to me read it to them.

TABLE OF CONTENTS

TABLE OF CONTENTS (cont.)

CHAPTER 1: THE TALKING DOLLS

Hi, I'm Dana. One day I was in my slippers and robe eating cereal. "But mom Ballet will be fun" I said. "Yes dear, but we can't afford it now" she said. I begged, cried, whined and pleaded but I guess it didn't work. "But Casandra is going" I said in a gurgling whine. "Yes, but you are not Casandra" she echoed my whine. I had no choice but to stomp up the steps to my room.

I have tons of pretty dolls with beady little eyes. When I go to bed they stare at me wickedly. I could almost hear them cackling in my head, puncturing my brain. I sweat all night! The next day was Monday, the worst day ever. I wake up at 6:43 and go to SCHOOL. I get packed and wait for the bus. My BFF Casandra sits with me. Emily and Hannah sit across from us chit-chatting about Webkinz and such. Kayla, the mean girl, sits in the very back like she always does. I heard Emily say, while she rolls her eyes, "She will always sit there because that's where the popular kids sit". When we hit school I overhear Kayla call me, Emily, Casandra and Hannah "dorks". So I turn around and give her the "evil look". "I'm totally like, the coolest kid here" she said in a cocky voice. I grab my backpack and head out the bus door.

When school ended, me and my friends walked out together because we're all going to a sleep-over at Emily's house. Everything was going well until I heard Kayla call out "Having a looser sleep-over?" "No, Frayla" I said back. "Ha-ha, very funny" she said in a louder fake cocky voice. "You remind me of my evil witch doll" I said back. "Oh yeah, well then, East, West, whose the best? Cast a spell on Dana!" Kayla said. I felt a cold shiver up my spine and everything was white! I saw a flashback of my dolls evil eyes!! I slept over at Emily's house and when I got home I did homework and ate dinner. When I went to bed I looked at my dresser and thought I saw a doll move! I blinked just to make sure it didn't move. I closed my eyes and I thought I heard a "pssst" in my ear. When I looked over and saw Mindy, my blonde doll, blinking right at me. I screamed as loud as possible.

CHAPTER 2: MINDY'S DINNER

"Hi" she said in a creepy but cute voice. "You smell like dinner when you die" she yelled wickedly. So I ran downstairs to get a drink of milk to cool off my brain. The next day of school I told my friends about Mindy. "Yeah right, what a weird dream". Hannah said. "But it wasn't a dream" I said. "Okay then explain the "die" part" Emily hollered back. "Well, well....well....well........um...uh... you're right, it was just my imagination" I cried back. We walked to our lockers together. "I can't believe Frayla, can you?" Hannah blurted out. I gulped hard, "yeah" I wobbled weakly. When I got home I lay on the couch. I felt like I was going to up-chuck. I went to get a drink of water. Emily came over to check on me. "How ya feelin? She asked. "Oh...uh...yah...juh....just fine" I whispered. Just then and there Mindy came down! "Oooh a feast for lunch and an appetizer!" she blurted. "Ah help us!!!" we hollered together as if one. "Run" I called out. We ran out the garage door. We blinked to see that we were not really having this happen to us. "Whew" Emily said, sounding like she couldn't catch her breath. "Hey want a 7-up?" I asked breathing hard. "Sure" she said opening the fridge door, we grabbed our sodas. "So, you weren't lying" Emily said, staring at the clock. "Told ya" I puffed out. The next day I asked Kayla if that was a real spell. "No, I just pretended to scare you "she said twisting her ponytail. "Casandra grab Dana's hand" Hannah yelled to Casandra. "Sure" Casandra said, reaching towards my hand. I squeezed her hand tightly. We walked to the 6th grade room. I let go of Emily's hand so she could feed the fish. Guppy and Bubbles were our fish's names. They are so cute! We arched into the room quietly and sweetly. We walked past the fat blackboard and we hung up our coats and backpacks. Hannah sat at her seat softly. Emily sat next to me, holding her pencil eraser at her cheek. Casandra sat next to Joe, biting her lip and closing her eyes. She picked up her chair, and then slashed it down on the floor. "OOOOOH, bad mood Bubba" Kayla laughed. "You fat jerk" Casandra said, rolling her eyes. "What did you just say freak?" Kayla flipped back. "You heard me" Casandra said "big fat jerk!" Kayla crouched down and put her face at Casandra's face and said "you listen to me and you listen good, you are the ugliest brat ever to walk the planet. Do you hear me?" "Yes SIR" Casandra giggled. She had the whole class dying laughing. "Knock it off with the jokes Miss so funny" Kayla said walking away.

CHAPTER 3: THE DOLL FIRE!

At home I played Dance, Dance, revolution with Hannah and Emily. Casandra had detention so she couldn't come. Hannah was really winning! When she left Emily and I climbed on rocks and up trees. We played soccer and swung on my play ropes. We also jumped rope, ate ice pops and jumped on the trampoline. Then we caught frogs and threw rocks in the river. Emily's mom came so I said bye to Emily. I went upstairs to my room and saw it was smoky and red! I heard crinkle crackles and my face was hot. Through the fog I could see high red, yellow, orange and black flames. I shut the door and ran to my mom. "Mom, Mom, Mom! Help, my room is on fire and it's burning down" I yelled to her. Her face became broad and serious. I ran up before her and when I opened the door my dolls were walking through the fire. "We've been waiting for you" my doll Chelsea said in an evil haunting voice. "Aaaaahhhh!" I yelled, my heart beating faster than anything in the world. I closed the door and my mom was running through the hall panting. "Hurry mom" I screamed. When she opened the door there was no smoke, no flame and no moving dolls. Just my old same, and clear, room. "I can explain there really was a fire. She slapped my hand "don't ever do that again, that's called 'crying wolf'" she said extra mad. "But I did choke on smoke and bright orange flames grew black and high" I whined, very upset. A smile grew big on Chelsea's face and then her pink lips turned back. Later on, the aroma of pizza filled the air. Casandra called on the phone and we talked and talked and talked for hours. We talked about Kayla, sports, webkinz, music and sleep-overs. I hung up nicely and sat at the dinner table with my mom and dad. My dad's hand shuffled thought his chocolate brown hair, then he reached for the soup. My mom pulled her light blonde hair in a short ponytail. I was so happy to see my dad because I didn't see him for 3 days. His job is a lawyer. I gave him a huge hug. I am an only child NOW because my older sister, Brooke, moved out because she is married. Her husband David is a Real Estate Agent at Washington town in Colorado. So Brooke moved there with him in an open-land house that is giant. Brooke works as a doctor there and it's near a doll store. She sends me lots of dolls. I gobbled through the pizza, soup and salad. I had some ice cream for dessert. I covered myself in my soft covers, relaxing. The next school morning I sat by Hannah playing games. In the beginning of school we have gym, so we played hockey and baseball. My team was Casandra, Eric, Hilary, Emily and Alayna. Kayla's team was Stacie, Hannah, Carly, Jalo and Cody. Kayla's team won in hockey but my team won in baseball. For snack I had cookies and oranges, but I kept having flashbacks about Chelsea and Mindy going to hurt me.

CHAPTER 4: THE MOUNTAIN BEAST FROM THE BOTTOM

I had to get that out of my system though Brooke told me to never give up and don't be afraid. So, if I work hard to clear my mind, Mindy or Chelsea won't haunt me. Tomorrow I go hiking in the mountains with my family. I can smell fresh grass, I can feel sun and rocks, I can see the Rocky Mountains high and low, and I can hear birds, bugs, wind and crunching. When I got home my mom was packing bags. She had so much stuff in one bag she had to sit on it! "Hey sweetie, can you sit on this and hold these books?" she asked, handing me a large pile of dictionaries. "Sure" I said. I bounced up and down, back and forth. My dad came down with a tape recorder, video camera and a camera. "Whoa, dad why do you need all that?" I asked staring at him. "Oh, I guess I didn't tell you, OK there is a beast in the mountain, with sharp claws, sharp teeth and he's very hairy. I want to catch every moment of him on these electrical babies!" he said as he held up his camera. "Cool! I wanna see him" I said excitedly. We were driving up to our cottage in the mountains. Rivers at the bottom flowed and the chimney on our cottage was teeming with smoke. Far from our mountain there were more purplish bluish pointy mountains that were snow-capped. A fat, broad-faced, smelly, ugly, old and buck toothed farmer with a pipe in his mouth welcomed us to the mountains. "You lookin for this cottage?" he asked. He sounded like a toad. He walked in and his bushy eyebrows were dusty. His finger turned the lights on, then he grabbed a long gun and plopped his chubby butt and belly on the sofa. "Yes sir this is the house." My dad said, zooming his camera. "I'm Mr. Fernredding." The fat man said with a grin. "Hey Mr. Fernredding, do you know about the hairy beast?" I asked slowly, I was looking at his 5 o'clock shadowed beard and mustache. "Know 'bout 'im? I've met the ugly dude myself" he said, like he was some great warrior. He spit a hack of tobacco in a can by the door. "How did you meet him" I withered, low and meek. Well, I's climbin those mountains and he popped up from behind a rock and clawed me." He said as he pulled his left pant leg up. It had a large red scar across from his knee cap to his ankle. "Hamburgers anyone?" he asked. "Sure", "Sure", "Sure". My mom, me and my dad said together. My mom came in again with bags. "Hey dad, do you think Mr. Fernredding is a little, oh I don't know, weird??" I said crazily. "Well sure he is he's 94." My dad said. I ran outside. A farm had a sign that read:

Olivia Oakley Peach Farm $2.00, I ran over with 8 quarters in my hand "Excuse me; um I'd like to buy a can of peaches please." I said kindly. A smile spread across the girl's face. "Why of course cutie." She said. She seemed so sweet. She handed me a peach can and I gave her the change. Just then I heard Mr. Fernredding squeal, "burgers are done!" I ran over to the cottage and began to eat my peaches. My dad poured water into a big cup and put out the fire. We ate in silence until mom asked "where did you get those?" she pointed to my peach can. "At that farm over there. They looked at the farm. I ran outside, I was ready for an adventure.

CHAPTER 5: THE GIRL WHO TALKS TO WIND

I climbed rocks, far away I saw it! A hair, a claw "Rawwww" the beast growled! "Get back here" he screamed, as I ran away. I hollered "help" but no one could here me! The beast plunged at me and put out his claw. He scratched my face hard and deep. Blood poured down my cheek. I opened my eyes to find myself on the couch with the television on. I ran to the kitchen and my mom was still making dinner. It was still Friday. I rubbed my cheek. No scratch! "fewww" I said in relief. I ran outside in my yard to play. Suddenly, lightning flashed, clouds grew gray, rain fell hard and thunder crackled. A deep voice from nowhere said "Dana, you must die". I stepped back and looked around. "Why me?" I asked shaking. "Because I am MINDY!!!" the wind yelled back. I screamed and ran to my doll Mindy. "Give me your necklace!" Mindy yelled loudly. "Ok, kay, kay, kay" I said. I ripped my beautiful necklace off my neck and handed it to her. "Thank you. Now I will send you back in time before my thunder started" Mindy said deeply. I was back where I started on the couch. "Wow" I squealed. A rainbow twinkle filled my eye.

I rubbed my eye. "Bluba bubbera" I blubbered, shaking my head around. All of a sudden a motor rumbled and fogged up the garage window. A fat lady with jet black hair was riding a yellow motorcycle with a bright orange helmet. She wore a dark blue shirt and light green capri's. She had Velcro flats and a shiny red visor. Her sparkly gemmed glasses were fat. My mom came out and started talking to the weird fat lady. I thought the lady was color blind. "Dana, this is Mrs. Hews." My mom introduced. "Ah, call me penny." The lady said shaking my hand. "I've come to buy the purple and green vase." Penny said, pointing to the door. She pulled out a wad of dollars. "Oh, right, yes, let me get it. My mom replied happily. "So do you like school?" she asked. "Yeah, I made a lot of friends" I said handing her a picture of my friends from the shelf. "Oh, their lovely" Penny said smiling. "thank you, that's very nice." I replied nicely. She smiled and said, "You're welcome. You know, I have 4 children, two boys and two girls." Penny said sweetly. "Cool" I said. "Here it is smooth and pretty" my mom said, holding the vase. "Oh just what I wanted" Penny said. She drove away and my mom and me went inside. Another knock on the door scared me to death. A dark skinned, blue eyed, black haired man walked in. He was not what caught my eye. His handsome son walked in. He had honey brown eyes, long blonde hair and light skin.

He was so cute. We were both 12 years old, so we could match up. He was like my grampa...wise, smart, heart-warming, strong and generous. When he shook my hand It felt like he swept me off my feet. I was in dreamland. He was like my father...fun-loving, wicked, crazy and talented. When he told stories he sounded mysterious and adventurous. When it was time for him to go my heart sank making me feel like a story and brat because I just met the dude.

CHAPTER 6: NINE TAILS, NIKKI & ME!

He shook my hand goodbye. I asked "Hey what's your last name." "Hews" he called back. "I'm Dana Heart singer." I said back. A shiver went up my spine, Hews, Hews, Hews why does that sound familiar? I went through the alphabet. I stopped at "P", "Penny Hews"! I screamed in my head. Mrs. Colorblind was Nikki's mama! Two days later, Nikki came back for a spring picnic with us. I took a walk with him by myself. We talked until I asked "Is your mom's name 'Penny'?" He silenced all fear when suddenly he answered "yes, I am her son." I wondered why that was so bad. Maybe because an accident or something. He handed me a blue rose. We walked further into the woods, where thorns got thicker and swamps grew gray and green. Dead flowers were squished in moss. The thorns hung over our heads and everywhere. Moss was as high as our knees. We talked more and laughed more. We heard a noise near us and we stopped in silence. A white furred, red eyed wolf/coyote stepped towards us. It color shifted and fire blasted at thorns. It quickly grew nine tails and hit me in the face with a fire blast. I fell to the ground and Nikki picked me up and ran with me in his arms. When we got to the bridge he put me down and I told him he couldn't tell anyone about this. I know the poor guy didn't understand what the heck was going on so he asked me. I told him, "I can't explain it. I know you are curious but it's a little much for a sensitive guy like you". We walked back to the picnic blanket to eat. Every now and then he would look up and smile at me. I would smile back and wave. We all ate 8 types of food: rice, chili, salad, buttered bagels, double chocolate chip cookies, strawberries, sunflower seeds and nacho burrito Frito chips. We all drank apple juice. It was a wonderful day for a picnic. Nature's sweet scent filled my nose and the suns warm rays bathed me. My dad pointed out a rainbow painted in the sky. It was so hot outside and we were all sweating. But, luckily a cool breeze cooled us down. Lilies sprayed the air and colorful dragonflies flew around. Dragon fruit grew everywhere around us. Chicklets began to sing sweet songs in harmony to the tune of 'A spoonful of sugar' from Mary Poppins, while bee's hummed 'zzzzzzzz' to the tune of "Going on 17' from the Sound of Music. I wanted so badly to sing along on a beautiful day like this humming 'Oh Suzanna', running towards the sun and washing my face in the pond. Just to feel my heartbeat. But, it would be impolite to cry aloud an old song and jump up in front of the Hew's.

This is much better than Colorado doll stores and stupid Real Estate agency signs with the ugly Drug Store Colorado Spring's first aid kits and popular 'Carrot Top' boarder signs. If I ever visit that cruddy place, I'll kill myself. I think that my opinion about Colorado being dumb is a fact. The only thing I like about Colorado is Brooke and probably those cute clothes signs with that pretty model Janine Angello. I'd like to see the Ice Age more than I would want to visit Colorado.

CHAPTER 7: COLORADO

But, I had to have my mind back to the romantic picnic before dusk when the moon splashes me in the face and starts winking with great delight. Day lilies and mint leaves sprouted out and filled the air with tropical chocolate mint aromas. Soon enough it was time for Nikki and his dad, Eric, to leave. Nikki said good-bye but then he shot me that look like 'should I kiss her?' then he bent over and the feeling of a kiss made my heart pound constantly. But then, he turned back and no lip-lock! I should've done it myself because soon we are visiting Brooke and David in Colorado so I won't see him in awhile. Hey, who says women can't propose? I had to measure up the total of: love Nikki measured against my BFF. Since I just met Nikki and he is a different gender his weight of measure was a little bit heavier than my friends. I really love Nikki with a passion but my friends are awesome and I've known them for years. I also need someone's shoulder to cry on and some bodies secrets to keep and a friendship to share. Which side cared more? Which side loved and knew the real me? Who would be there for me when I am sad or ill? And who would pick me up when I am down or hurt? "Well, Colorado, yep David, Brooke, Carrot Top, dolls and the Springs." I said as I boarded the plane to Colorado. My mom brought gum and small Dixie cups™ for my ears so they would not pop. I brought food, toys, games and my Nintendo DS™. All I thought about was the adorable Nikki. Is he hanging out with another girl cuter and prettier than me? Yes or no? I had to measure that up too. I smelled a thick aroma of paint and peanut butter crackers. A puffy red haired lady stood in front of the cockpit with an air bag, a seatbelt and a microphone "I guess she is the Flight Attendant" I whispered to my mom, as I eyed up her purple girly tuxedo. "Yeah, doncha see her seat belt that looks exactly like ours?" she asked, chewing away some Hubba Bubba™ gum. As our plane was getting ready for take-off, I had to lean back. I felt like a metamorphic rock because of the pressure. I took a deep breath and kept saying in my head "I am going to Colorado" over and over again. We shot up into the sky like a firecracker or a missile. As we flew up into the clouds I felt like playing tic-tac-toe or bingo with my mom or dad but my mom was reading a long chapter book and my dad was listening to his ipod™ to pass the time. A kid that was about 4 or 5 was kicking the back of my seat and this 9 year old boy in front of me kept turning around to look at me because he thought I was cute. The kid in front of me reminded me of Nikki, because he just gave you a cute smile of love, pride and joy. It just made me smile back. I could kill to see a smile like that every day. Just the way it felt inside me was marvelous. The kid had Mike Musso and Jason Dolley hair. His skin made him look like he was black. I looked out my window. We were so high up, the towns looked very tiny. It looked like I could pick them up! Teeny tiny!

CHAPTER 8: WHY DO YOU HATE ME?

When we landed in Colorado from Charlotte I saw thousands of amazing things at the airport there. From behind a casino wall and a corndog stand, I could see Brooke's pretty pace. "Brooke!" I yelled. I ran past the corndog vendor, missing the flying squirt of ketchup, I pushed David aside and gave Brooke a big squeeze. "Hey sis!" I said looking up at her. What's up cutie?" she asked, giving me a kiss. "Nothing, just pushing through the crowd to find you." I said, staring at all the people in the place. "How old are you anyway, 6?" David said smiling. "No dufus, I'm 12" I said cockily. David was reaching for his pocket of sour patch kids, when I caught him and asked "can I have some?" "NO!" David said meanly. Brooke punched him in his arm. "Davy, love!" Brooke said, handing me two sour people. "Thank you David." I said, sounding so innocent. David drove us home. Brook slept in the bed with David, Mom slept on the couch with dad and I brought my sleeping bag to sleep on the floor. Sleeping on the floor made me feel poor, lonely and sad. It was really cold down there. But, the good thing about it was it was easy to get up, so every now and then I could spy on Brooke and David, and I could fix myself up a snack when I'm hungry. I noticed they had grits, muffins (chocolate chip), eggs (hard-boiled) and a drawer that said, KEEP OUT! The drawer was filled with tons of jars of candy and desserts. A cabinet read: Olivia Oakley & Lily Owens. I peered inside. The side with Olivia Oakley on it had thousands of jars of peaches. The side with Lily Owens on it had tons of jars of honey wrapped very prettily. Olivia Oakley: from the mountains. Lily Owens: from the story 'Secret Life of Bees! I couldn't imagine what the honey tasted like. I quietly grabbed a jar and opened it with a sharp bread knife. I ate the whole thing with my finger. I threw the jar of honey away. I wrapped myself in my sleeping bag cover and tried to think of the feeling, 'cause I was to excited about spying that I couldn't go to sleep. I set up five porridge bowls for cereal tomorrow morning. I was the last one to wake up in the morning and I noticed every one was eating out of the exact bowls I wanted them to! Mom had purple, dad had blue, Brooke had pink and David had white. But, to my surprise, I wasn't left out. Brooke handed me a rainbow bowl and a heart spoon! Here, the best bowl for the best person ever. Thank you for setting out our bowls for us 'lil sis!" she said nicely. Everyone gave me a hug except for David. "Hey David, give her a hug." Brooke said. "I don't want this stupid bowl" David yelled out. "Why do you hate me?" I said. I ran out to the porch with my crocs on and cried on the porch rail. My teardrops just wouldn't stop pouring down so much. My face became bright red and puffy.

CHAPTER 9: I WON'T TELL

Brooke came out to comfort me. "I remember when we lived in Portugal and when we made pancakes, singing "oh, Susanna" with Gramma, and dad would tell us stories about fictions and back-then folk tales." Brooke said hugging me. "You mean fire talking?" I said snuffling. "Yea, like Fire talking" Brooke said. We watched the birds fly. The last teardrop fell and landed on the hotel patio. "You see how far that drop went? That's as long as you will live to be strong and sweet." Brooke said as she pointed to the wet drop splashing on the tar and rolling into the fresh grass. It started to rain and get cloudy. She handed me a bonbon chocolate caramel cluster. We split it and chewed it slowly to cherish the memory because we haven't had one in years. Then we watched a chubby rat sneak into the hole in the wall. Then out loud together we sang 'Oh! Susanna' and we sat on the porch rocking chair, rocking back and forth switching from 'Oh! Susanna' to 'A spoonful of sugar' and eating bonbons until we were sick. Our sisterhood would never end. "Brooke, I sort of hate David, and he is mean to me" I broke out. "Please don't

tell him!" I said. "I won't tell. I won't breathe a word"
Brooke said. I could tell she meant it because her
words twisted in my head and tickled me. She was an
awesome friend and a wise sister. She held my hand
and we walked into the house so late it was lunch!! I
listened to Brooke play the harp to the tune of the
church psalm 'Here I am Lord' in a beautiful sound
that made my heart sing. For a snack, mom, Brooke
and I ate cookie straws, while dad and David google
searched about ipods and guy stuff. We watched
'Sponge Bob' until dad put on stupid CSI for 3 hours.
I guess I got used to comedy Central after watching
72 clips for 10 hours straight because David likes
that dumb channel because of Charlie Murphy and
Eddie Griffin. We watched too much of 'Rocky' and
now the song 'Eye of the Tiger' is stuck in my head.
I was reaching for the salt on the high shelf but I
knocked down the pepper and it came pouring down
on my head. "Oh my gosh" "Shut up!" my mom said
picking up the pepper jar. Brooke dusted me off. I
took a very long shower that night. I thought about
how soon I was going to see Nikki... three more days!
How mean David was made Nikki seem so much nicer
to me. As hours passed, David and I became good
friends. I wanted to kneel down and kiss Brooke's
feet for what she did for me on the porch. David
became very playful and fun with me. He made me

feel a special way. A way so special I am now glad to say 'that's my brother in law'. Hanging out with boys and being around a lot of girls made me half male and half female. Finally we had a night of a lot of talking, tonight. I sat in the middle of Brooke and mom. Mom sat between me and dad, and Brooke sat between David and me. What made the table so sad was when I passed David the salad with cranberries and nuts in it. David forgot he's allergic to cranberries and he gobbled down the salad. He said "I feel sick, excuse me." He walked into the bathroom. Brooke walked in and noticed he was throwing up. I watched him come back to the room. "Oh my gosh David, you have hives!

CHAPTER 10: DAVID HATED CRANBERRIES

David chokes until Brooke remembers that David is allergic to cranberries. My dad and Brooke drove David to the hospital called, Janders Town General Hospital. I stayed at the house with mom. I felt so bad for David. Even though I'm the one who's allergic to daffodils and toadstool mushrooms. I paced back and forth just wondering what was happening to David right now. What is he suffering? Is he ok? Is he seeing stars? I read some 'Highlights' books to pass the time. His last three words when he stepped in the car were "I'll be ok". Yea right, that crazy guy could be dying right now and he is saying he's ok. What the heck was that guy talking about? Sometimes I think he knows he is stupid but he won't admit it. He's as dumb as a pencil eraser. I ate some choco bits to calm me down but I waited five hours for him to come back and I'm not waiting anymore. "Lets go to the hospital mom!" I shouted. "NO! Be patient he'll be ok and he'll come back soon!" she shouted back to me. Well now what was I gonna do? I can't take a space ship! Janders Town was 32 miles away. I'm not gonna walk there, I mean come on how long could it take for him to like, get an inspection, get medicine and leave! I could do that myself in twenty minutes. I'm probably faster than the medical slow geeks down at the junk yard. I stood on the porch looking down below to see if any red Ford trucks were parking in our garage, well in Brooke and David's garage. I was so tired. I wanted to go to sleep but I wanted to see David come back looking better. I looked up at the pizza clock. It had '10:59' on it. I had bags under my eyes and black circles around eyes. I came in side the house to sit and watch 'Hannah Montana'. I did everything that was loud to keep me occupied and keep me from dozing. I tried playing Brooke's harp real loud. I turned up the volume to 106 on the TV and when I listened to my ipod, I turned it up to volume 116. Finally a car pulled in and Dad, Brooke and David walked in. David looked a lot better than before. "What took you guys so long? I am so tired" I said. "Good night" everyone called to me. I snuggled in my sleeping bag. I didn't mind that no one turned the air conditioner off so I was freezing to death. The next day we had breakfast and went on the plane to go home. I took a chapter book to read on the way called 'The Mystery of the ghost in the Wall'. I played a game of Link'd with my mom and a game of 'go fish' with my dad. I didn't sit in front of the five-year-old kicking kid and the Nikki look-alike sat across from me. I had the seat next to the cock-pit so I could see inside and the perfect view of the plane TV. Since I was in the front seat I was the first to get my snack and drink from the cart. When we stopped in Charlotte and we went to the "Rainforest Café" which is the coolest café in the world.

CHAPTER 11: TRUE LOVE KISS

When we landed in Pennsylvania, Nikki welcomed us home. I ran to him giving him a big hug. Just then, I felt the kiss feeling again. He bent down and.....KISS!! Love filled the air. TRUE LOVES KISS! I knew it would happen sometime if not, sooner. Penny was there to give me a hug... Emily stood there with a present. I gave her a big hug. Casandra's whole family came with cards and presents and I gave her a huge hug. Hannah showed up with a card and a $50 bill in it! I gave her a big squeeze. My Grama stood there with cards, presents and a check for $1,000. I squeezed her tightly. I put my head on Nikki's shoulder as he held me and my friends gave me a group hug. A sunset shone brightly, as we drove home. we held a 'welcome back' party and invited everyone. We ate and had fun. When we swam in the pool Nikki and me fought. "I can dive" I said. "Can not" Nickki teased. "Uh-huh" "Nu-uh" back and forth until I did one and splashed him in his face. "Hey" he laughed as he splashed me back. "Uh-oh" I yelled. "kaboom " Emily cannon balled into the pool. Aside from the sponge cake, cards, pool and yummy food, I got to open my presents and keep the money. I counted my money... $50 + $1,000 + $50 +$100 = 1,200. Colorado made me feel lucky. But in Pennsylvania, you might as well name me lucky! What makes me lucky? Nikki, my cool friends, $1,200, my own clubhouse, an awesome big sister, my cool family and my awesome red hair color that goes down to my ankles. I wonder why Nikki likes me. I think I am ugly except for my hair. My friends say I am pretty but maybe they mean my hair. Maybe Nikki saw what's inside of me? I am the star pupil. And I'm really really smart. I'm sporty so I proved that girls can do anything. I'm kind, like I tend to plants and I love animals. I'm different, maybe that's why Nikki likes me. When Nikki, Casandra, Hannah and I went inside we heard a noise in my room. We climbed up all the mansion/house steps to my room. A rainbow was splashed under my bed. My friends and I stood back as Nikki peeked under my bed. The rainbow disappeared as soon as Nikki put his knees to the floor. He looked under and....NOTHING! Casandra looked under.....NOTHING! Hannah looked under....NOTHING! "Rats" Hannah yelled. Then Nikki and I noticed the missing piece to the puzzle, true love needs to do it together! So we both bent down together and.... A BOOK! A book I never had before. It was gold, brown and green. Nikki blew on it because it was dusty. Together, aloud, Nikki and I carefully read it, "Raja Island".

CHAPTER 12: THE PORTAL TO RAJA ISLAND

"Raja Island" we said together. Suddenly, a purple swirly portal arrived inside the window. We all stepped inside with Nikki holding the book. Unaware of the cold mist from the foggy portal, we pushed and pulled to fit inside. Then one by one we carefully stepped into the other world. We ended up in a sticky sand beach and an ocean rushed up to touch our feet. We stepped forward into the palm tree safari beach jungle. Nikki opened up the book to find a path direction. The first page of the book read, "Red path, Blue path, guess which one? Follow the owl sounds then you'll be done." My friends and I noticed it rhymed. We listened carefully to hear any owl hoots but all we heard was cooing. "cuooing-HmHmmmm," "It sounds like an owl" Casandra screamed, pointing to the blue path which had the strange bird cooing like an owl. We ran through the path until we noticed a puddle of quick sand with ruby red snakes surrounding it. About four of them hissed until Nikki showed them the book. Then one spoke "You sssir can not have that book of our Island. We need it for our Emperor Rani and King Raja. We will give you help of the next riddle if you tear out that page and let usss have it. To give to Rani. We will tell you the sssecret to the page you tore out." "Ok, what's your name" Nikki asked, tearing out the page. "Yasssmin" she answered so slowly. "Hi, I'm Nikki" he answered. "Yesss, now we will tell you the sssecret. The Ginger pond will ask you for 3 lilies, pink, orange and blue. The pink is actually red, here isss the orange one for you and the blue one is behind the huge maple tree". Yasmin said. We took the orange one and ran, The Ginger pond did exactly what Yasmin said and we took her directions like she was a commander. We walked ahead and I thought we were done, but Pyramids were scattered around and Boonas were holding Pharaohs. The Raja Island was the land of gods and goddesses. Egyptian wall painting was cool, but they had more than that. I like the pictures of Cleopatra. The mummies made me jump but it was funny how they looked like cone heads, just walking around like babies holding out their hands. I could smell a trashy stench of coffee. A place like this was magical. I listened to the Boonas play bongo drums and Egyptian flutes. We walked ahead and the music became faster. We walked up to a pyramid, just climbing it made me want to barf. We took steps inside. "Oh my gosh! Nikki, I can't see" Emily shouted. Nikki grabbed a lit torch to lead the way. We went though the warm, dark tunnel with Nikki and me leading the way. We peered out the caged pyramid windows to look at the blue deer. Inside the pyramid was gold and dust, but that didn't affect us at all. The Cleopatra pictures could fall, they look so loose.

CHAPTER 13: BOONAS ARE RELIGIOUS?

As we walked further I noticed some golden cows. "Why the heck do they have statues of silver cows?" Emily wondered. "They're not silver you bonehead, they're gold!" Hannah shouted. "Break it up guys. Silver or gold, the question is why do they have cows?" Casandra yelled, breaking them up. I think cows, ah golden cows had to do with Moses, didn't it?" I said, trying to remember religion classes on Moses. "Yea! Your right Dana!" Nikki said. "OH MY GOSH! The Boonas are RELIGIOUS!" Emily screeched. "Hey won't my mom think we're dead somewhere?" I asked Nikki. "No, I wrote her a note saying 'Dear Mrs. Heartsinger, we're at the store buying stuff, so we might be late, Your friend, Nikki." Nikki said. I am so glad Nikki's my boyfriend. I put on some Burt's Bees chap stick. We came to a long, twisty, golden slide that was as skinny as about six or seven water bottles put together. Casandra slid down first singing a song called 'I love you' by the Robotic Electrics Band. Then Hannah went zooming down, screaming. Next, Emily went flying down. Then it was my turn. I zipped and zoomed on every curvy turn. My long hair flew around everywhere! I whipped around and dust would puff every where. I started to hear Nikki sliding down behind me. I could hear his cape whipping around in the air, snapping. I looked back to see him but it was too dark to see anything. I hit the ground with a large "THUMP!" I bounced on the sand like a bungee string. A blue skinned cowboy with a red cowboy suit and a tall black cowboy hat picked me up by the hand. He was a honky-tonk guy and a red neck, even though his skin was blue. My friends and I watched 8 purple polar bears plunge off of a yellowish, orangey, reddish iceberg. I tied my left shoelace. The cowboy told us to go in the woods so we did. We were very cautious because it was dark and we didn't want to bump into anything bad. It was cold and it smelled like fish. The harsh fog made it hard for us to breathe. Nikki held me close, Casandra held mine and Emily's hands. Hannah held Nikki's other hand. We heard ropes tumble down from the sky. Pirates, scarred and bruised, dropped down from the ropes and their shiny swords glistened in the fog, they swung their swords around. Nikki grabbed a long, sharp stick to fight swords with them. Hannah, Emily, Casandra and I did karate moves against them. Just then, there was one pirate left and he made a cut on Nikki's arm with his sword. So I ripped off the pirate's nose. The pirate ran away. I cleaned Nikki's cut with pond water. The rocks that stuck up from the ground looked like the tops of knives. There were rotted apple trees along the way. Casandra was shaking and Hannah's teeth were chattering.

CHAPTER 14: JERRY THE HIPPO

As we walked, Casandra scarcely noticed a hippo walking out of the swamp. "Um, excuse me sir, how do we get out of here?" Emily screamed running and wailing towards the hippo. He smiled and walked back to us. He started to yell and he sounded sort of like an ambulance horn. He stopped at our feet, "The name's Jerry, Jerry Fishman." he said. He sounded like a dopey guy. "Hey, yea, hi, um, do you know how to get out of here?" Nikki asked. "Nope, I've lived here all my life." Jerry said, disappointed he couldn't help us. "Oh, well thanks anyway." I said sadly. "You're welcome, sorry and good luck. Jerry said. We walked along the checkerboard like path. The beat of 'East Northumberland High' by Miley Cyrus was in my head as we passed scary shadows and noises. A brown door was in the middle of the path, floating and glowing. Shaking and sweating, I slowly opened the door. It was pitch black. When we all walked in, a purple sparkly thing scooped us up and pulled us down. "Ahhhhh" we all screamed. We landed on my roof, just a stone's throw from the window. We all jumped over to the window except Hannah. "Come on Hannah". I yelled. "NO way, I'm terribly afraid of heights. I'm already freaked out" she said terrified. "Just trust me, you know you can do it" I called to her. She grabbed on and I squeezed tightly. Emily grabbed my waist and pulled. Casandra grabbed Emily's waist and pulled. We were making a chain! Nikki reached out and grabbed Hannah's other hand. Hannah leaped and finally we were all at my window. We ran downstairs. "Whew, the parents are still outside." Casandra said happily. "Yeah but we have to act like we ere at Winn Dixie store" I said. My mom walked in holding papers that were folded. "Hey Dana and Emily, you girls are signed up for gymnastics at Cartwheel with Carla!" My mom said with a broad smile. "WHAT?" Emily asked. "Yeah your mom and I called and got you girls signed up" my mom answered Emily. I was going to gymnastics, and with my 2nd best friend! "Cool!" I said in embarrassment. I was embarrassed because Emily was terrified. She was terrified because she hates gymnastics. The trampoline scares her the balance beam scares her because of the height, the bars scare her because once she tried them and broke her arm and nose AND the air track scares her because it is way too bouncy. The next day, Emily and I had to wear leotards. We were going to gymnastics. When we entered Cartwheel with Carla, it was huge. I mean it was really HUGE!

CHAPTER 15: THE HAUNTED GYMNASTICS CLASS

We looked around. We saw a sponge pit, a double mini tamp, a trampoline, an air track, a spring floor, bars, 3 beams and 5 gymnast teachers. Emily squeezed my hand and we walked forward to the teachers. "OK, we'll start with the pit" Miss Carla announced. "Whew, at least it's something easy and fun" Emily said to me with a pink face. "Let's bounce off the air track into the pit" Carla said nicely. "Oh no! I hate the air track, I'll ask for another option" Emily said scared "Um, Miss Carla can I just run across the air track into the pit?" Emily asked nicely. "Sure, whatever" Carla answered rolling her eyes. "OK, great, yeah, thanks!" Emily said meanly. We started at the air track. I was the first to go in. I did a front flip in and landed very softly. When I landed I was surrounded by blue cheese-like squares. Then, a cold plastic hand grabbed my ankle! And another hand grabbed my wrist! The hands sucked me down to the trampoline, and then past it, to the bottom. I struggled and tried holding my breath. The sponge's corner was in my mouth, I couldn't breathe any longer. I was being suffocated by what I think was Mindy. Luckily, a warm soft hand pulled me up higher and the cold hands let go of me. I was pulled up to safety by Emily and I could breathe again! Parents and adults clapped and cheered as Emily and Mrs. Dawn pulled me up the steps to my mom. "Alright that's probably enough gymnastics for you girls" Emily's mom said, hugging me and Emily. "Let's go to Iceez for some ice-cream" my mom said. Grabbing the snack bag and heading down the other steps. "Alright" I exclaimed, slapping Emily a high-five. We drove to Iceez. There was a park there so I played at the playground park with Emily after I finished my chocolate chunk mocha ice cream. It began to get dark. The moon was glowing so brightly, it was yellow. It was getting cold and I had goose bumps. The sky was starry. "Ok kids, it's getting cold, I think we should be getting home" my mom said. "Yeah you guys have homework to do" Emily's mom added, scarfing down a chocolate toffee ice cream sandwich. Tomorrow was Friday, soccer practice. When I got home, I did my homework, of course and went to bed. It was hot, and I don't mean hot, I mean HOT! I was red, hot and my covers were all ripped off.

CHAPTER 16: WITCHY WATER!

In the middle of the night I was woken by my nightmare. So, I was awake for twenty minutes watching my quiet house's roof and listening to the ticking of the clock on the wall. My heart was pounding. I never had such a scary dream before. The next morning I went to school and was standing by the shiny grayish, silver bleachers, near the cheerleaders. So far, we were winning the soccer game! I glanced at the scoreboard: 5 to 2. The lunch bell rang in the middle of our sixth goal. Emily and Casandra caught up with me. Hannah was holding the ball in her hand. We entered the school doors and sat down in our chairs. The teacher carefully wrote pronouns on the board. Trisha raised her hand "Um, the recess bell just rang" she said. "Oh, yes, um I guess you're right" the teacher replied. When I got home that day my mom said, "Wanna go to the Waldensburg water park?" "Well sure who's going?" I asked. "Hannah and Trisha" she answered. "Ok, I'll go" I said. I wore my bathing suit and got in the car. When we got there, Hannah was sitting on a red bench. I walked up to her. "sup? I'm in my watery hiz house" Hannah said, looking at the pool. "Shut up" I said, rolling my eyes. "Where's Trisha? She should be here by now" I said. "Why?" "'Cause she lives across the street/" "Really?" "Yeah, duh!" I said back. "C'mon, let's just go swimming" I said, running through some sprinklers! "Ok" Hannah answered, tugging her glasses off her head. We walked to the deep end and I slowly walked/balanced myself on the diving board. I did three bounces while I closed my eyes. And....BOING! "Cannon Ball" I screeched. Splash! Into the water. Something sharp scraped my foot. Cackles swarmed around me and more sharp things stabbed me. I was bleeding! Someone grabbed me and pulled me out of the water! Hanna! People crowded me, I started crying very hard "Well, that's enough" my mom said. "What's going on with you and sports?" My mom cleaned the cuts with a first aid kit. That made me feel better, a whole lot better! It stung a little but it was worth it. "Are you OK?" Hannah asked, scarfing down a cheese pizza. "Yeah, I'm fine" I answered glancing up at her sauced-up face. Now she was sucking down her Dr. Pepper.

CHAPTER 17: LILLIAN JOHNSON

"Hey Dana! Over by the gates" someone called. "Hey (hay) is for horses!" Hannah called back helping me up off the bench. My legs were too wobbly to get up. "Shut-up! It's me Emily" Emily wailed back. My eyes widened and I stood straight up. I felt a lump form in my throat. It was her and she was here! "Emily" I called. I tried running but....ow ow ow. "Ouch, that's gotta hurt" Hannah said covering on eye. "Well don't just stand there, help me Hannah" I screeched. "Oh, yeah, sorry" she apologized, picking me up and carrying me slowly to Emily. "I said help me up not carry me like a baby!" I said smiling. Emily giggled and Hanna tried to hold her laugh in. "Ha Ha" we all laughed out loud rolling on our stomachs. "Come on, let's go Dana" my mom said, holding my jacket. "Why?" I complained. "Because we are going to the adoption center" she explained. The adoption center? Why in the world were we going there? "Oh yeah, OK fine" I whimpered. We drove to the adoption center, listening to 'Shake it'. 'Here we are" I said to myself. When we got there I immediately noticed the pink and white tile steps that go up to the cherry wood castle-like door. Mom and I walked in, kids surrounding us and playing with each other. Mom walked to the adoption desk. "I'm here" Mom's voice trailed off from the sounds of screaming girls running from a boy who looked about seven years old. I pushed my way through the crowd of little people to follow mom into a scraggly, old-looking door that read: Children. I was scared. Was my mom sending me here? Didn't she want me? When the door opened, it made a screeching sound and it looked like the woman had to struggle and push very hard, just to open the small, old, smelly door. When I stepped inside, I noticed a small, pretty, cute, little girl, with wavy, shoulder length, bouncy hair. Her hair color was bright red mixed with thin strands of electric blonde highlights. Her skin was medium and her face was spotted with red and brown freckles. She stood straight with her hands behind her back and her pointed chin up. Her eyes twinkled from the shine of the old, small lights that looked almost blinding. The room felt small and cramped with creaky floors and a ceiling with brown dents (even when the ceiling was white). The girl's t-shirt was orange, pink and white. And her shorts were pink and wrinkly. Her nails were painted bright hot pink. "Her name is Lillian and FYI she's my B.F.F." a little girl with thick lensed glasses and a crazy hairstyle said, balling hysterically. "What's wrong" I asked the girl, placing my hands on her slender shoulders. "I'll, I....I ...I'll miss her!" she cried, her face red and wet. "You mean she's going home with me?" I asked. "Yeah, you should know" she said, wiping her face and sniffing a nose full of tears and snot. That's when it hit me, mom wasn't giving me away, we were taking Lillian home! Whoopee, another sister! Good bye only child. What would Mom and Dad name her? "Lillian, your new name is Casity and this is your new mom and your sister." The clerk said, handing mom some papers. "Hello, I'm your new sister. I can't wait!" I said. "Hi, I know who you are, your Dana Heartsinger. We're going to be B.F.F.W.G.S.A.S.!" she said quickly. She talked really fast for a seven year old. I wondered what B.F.F.W.G.S.A.S. meant. Just then, I spied a giant spider the size of a play-pit ball, climbing up my swimming shoe! "Yeek!" I screeched, I jumped up and down and tried fluffing it off. "It's just a little spider. This place is so old, we have those and more crawling things in here. One went in my croc, I wasn't afraid. Did you know spiders have eight legs? I do! My friend Anika told me. She knows everything! Shawna is my B.F.F. She's really smart." She blabbered. That's way more than enough! I hated spiders and I really didn't want to hear or know anything else about them. Oh and my biggest fear is scorpions. Who likes scorpions? My mom signed a few papers, then she took Lillian (Casity) by the hand and said, "Come on

Dana, Cassy is ours to keep". 'Cassy' was that her nickname? Probably! I held Casity's hand because mom said so. As we walked, I noticed cobwebs in corners of the rooms. I saw a few kids whimpering, crying and moaning. Even staring in terror! Just frozen there in horror. A two year old was forcing out a minor cry, a ten year old was majorly sobbing and a five year old was crying wildly. I noticed a baby saying "y, yian" over and over. Casity walked over to the baby and said through tears, "I'll miss you the most Madeline". She cried and cried, hugging and kissing the baby girl. I felt like crying out loud. She must have rally loved that tiny, little baby. I felt horrible. We walked to the car. Casity still crying and me with tears streaking down my face. When we buckled in, Lillian/Casity asked "w..w..w...what do I..I huh..sniff, do?" "I'll H..h..help you, sniff" I offered my help to the little girl with the coolest, wickedest hair I ever saw. "Thanks b..b..big D" she said. Big D, I looked up at her beautiful face loaded with freckles, she stared up at me, then we started laughing so much, we couldn't even breathe! "Ah yeah, Big D, that's a good one. Aha a ahaah, sniff oh yeah." She giggled stiffening up her back then letting it curve and droop her shoulders down. When I stopped laughing, I buckled Casity in and made sure it was tight. She may be talkative but she could be my best friend in the world. The thought made me smile and stare into space, thinking of holidays, celebrations and the fun we would have together. Emily, Casandra and Hannah could come over and brag about her being better at something than them, like checkers, soccer, hide-and-go-seek, video games, running, swimming or dance, dance revolution. She could tell the best scary stories and wear the best costume on Halloween. Decorate the best Christmas tree at Christmas time, find the most Easter eggs at Easter, be the best pupil in school and write the best Valentine on Valentine's Day. I could be really popular in school and she could have kids fighting over her to be her best friend in school. But, like mom said, she's ours to keep.

CHAPTER 18: THE CAMPING SLEEP-OVER

We drove home. I couldn't wait for dad to see Casity. He probably already knows but he doesn't know what she looks like! The ride home was fast and we swiftly unbuckled "Dad, Dad, look what I got" I yelled. He couldn't see us but he could hear us. "Another Toy?" he called. "Sort of, but even better" I hollered. He came into view. Yes! Oh yeah! "Casity! Your home!" he yelled happily, picking her up, tickling her and stroking her very wavy hair. "She's here" Mom said. We got inside, had dinner and when I got upstairs, mom and dad surprised Casity and me with a gorgeous pink bunk bed. "I call sleeping up top" I said. I quickly remembered I roll around at night. "Oops, I forgot I roll around too much at bedtime" I said again. "OK sleeping on top will be fun. I can tell my new friends that I sleep on the top bunk" she giggled, tossing a frilly pink pillow and a big fat squishy frog up top. The frog was the most bloated thing ever saw. Casity climbed the hot pink wooden ladder. Sucking her thumb, she made the tall climb all the way to the top. She was still sucking on her thumb and now chewing on the sucked thumbs long pointy nail. Eww gross! I hopped in bed and put the Hannah Montana sheets that were warm, over my cold body and long red hair. At dinner I found out a lot about Casity. The next day, I woke up at 10:45 AM. "Oh no, I'm late for school" I yelled/whispered, catching a whiff of chocolate chip pancakes. Mom never makes pancakes on school days. I climbed up the ladder and noticed Casity was gone. The sheets were pulled back. I climbed down the ladder and ran down the steps as fast as I could. "Mom, Casity is go…" I began, but stopped as I saw Casity setting up dads tray with a napkin, knife and a plate stacked with pancakes. "She's right here honey. Mom smiled. "Well anyway I'm late for school." I said. "Oh, yes. I see. Well your sister is having a camping sleepover. Do you want to come? I told Principal Tomms that you wouldn't be in school because of your new sister. Emily, Hannah and Casandra are invited, so they cut school too! "Yahoo! No school, camping sleepover, decorating my new sister's 8th birthday party. This could be the best day ever. We decorated the house with a camping theme and set up a huge blue tent in the backyard and flags with symbols on them describing what the place is. It was really fun. "Thanks for helping out for my party" Casity said as the doorbell rang. "That's them! I can't wait come on Dana" Casity said, very excitedly. "Come on Sissy" she said again. Sissy, as in sister? "Sissy?" I questioned her, staring into her big brown hazel and blue eyes. "Yeah, you know like sister. It's Sissy for short. Libby told me to call my new sister that. Libby is the ten year old that I said goodbye to" Casity answered quickly. We ran to the garage door, through the house and to the door. The whole time I was thinking of having a little sister that called me 'Sissy'. It would be great. Mom answered the door. "Hi, where's Casity? Is all my friends would ask. "She's right here" I said quietly and meekly. Everyone ran to her saying how cute she is and making a fuss over her. "Guys, your goody bags are on the table. Mom and I worked all night doing them" Casity said proudly. "Great" Hannah said looking them over. "I call having the orange and green cup" Emily shouted to Hanna and Casandra, who were racing over to get a good bag and a fudge cookie. "I love your hair. It's so wicked. I mean I love the electric blond!" Emily said in amazement, glancing up at me. I tied the knot on my pink homemade sewn sweater, even tighter. Saliva foam was fizzing up in my mouth. I couldn't wait till cake! It looked so real and delicious. I helped mom bake and Casity picked the topping and decorated it with mini tents made out of candy, ho-hos and a whole ton more. "Let's do some games. Mom suggested. "Sure" everyone answered together. "Come on outside everybody, Dana helped me set up" Casity giggled. We walked to the back screen door, my friends following Casity everywhere she went. When we got outside, Casandra said, "Wow this place looks like a real campsite." "Thank you, Sissy and I tried the best we could and...." Casity started, but was interrupted by Hannah. "Sissy? Who's Sissy?" she asked. "Ahem, that's my title." I said proudly. "No it's not" She bickered. "To Casity it is" I screamed. Just as I finished, mom announced, "Let's throw fake darts in to the grass." We had thick cover of masking tape on the points so that no one got hurt. The object of the game was to throw it the farthest. To be funny we all showed each other our muscles and puffed out our cheeks while we did. Casandra was the first. "Come on Casandra, you can do it!" Casandra's mom yelled. Her mom was so pretty and her dad was always fun with us. He loved being funny. Casandra pulled the dart back, the feathered end past her shoulder, ZIPP! There is went, whizzing past dad who was the keeper, the one who keeps the scores. It went pretty far. Casity was up; it took her a long time to throw.... but it was worth it. It went way, way; past Casandra's and landed into the woods at the end. "Wow" all my friends and I said, staring in amazement. She was really good, a few games past and it came time for cake. Everyone gobbled it down. By then it was 8:34. We told some super scary stories, while we sat on our benches around the fire, roasting hot dogs and smores. We had our flashlights, stuffed animals and shared blankets while we snuggled close, listening to dad's scary stories. Dads were really scary! But Casity told the best stories. We were all scared to death with hers. After the fire stories and such, we all went inside the tent, huddled close together in our sleeping bags. This was a really cool idea. We all heard freaky noises and saw creepy shadows. Zzzz the next morning was awesome. We played sleeping bag games in the tent from 3:00 to 4:56. For breakfast we had eggs, bacon, toast and orange juice. Some kids had cereal, chocolate milk or chocolate chip muffins. It was so much fun. All my friends left with their goody bags.

CHAPTER 19: CASITY-STIEN

After my friends left, my family had a usual family night. Mom asked, "Halloween is coming soon girls, what you want to be?" Casity and I looked at each other for a moment. "I want to be a zombie bride" I said excitedly. Casity thought long and hard. "I could be, Frankenstein". She laughed. Mom and I started cracking up! Dude, you'd be like, Casitystein!" I bubbled. We all laughed so hard. The rest of the night I called Casity 'Casitystien'. After awhile, something terrible happened. "Aaaahhhh!!!!!" screamed Casity as loud as possible. "What? What? What's the matter?" I asked droop-eyed. When I got to the top of the ladder, Mindy had Casity in a rear choke hold (otherwise, a choke-out move). "Help me Sissy!" she choked out. I tried ripping Mindy's solid hands off Casity's neck but I couldn't. "There's no way you can save Casitystien now!" Mindy screeched. She must have thought Casity's name was Casitystien since I called her that earlier tonight. Mindy's plastic grip grew tighter. Pop! Mindy's fake doll arm popped off! There was my cue! I grabbed Casity and hopped off the bed, down the carpeted steps we ran. We panted loudly, Casity's hand was still locked in mine, her nails digging into my skin. Our slippers were thumping loudly and our chests were hot. Mindy was still chasing after us. Pop! There goes the right leg! "Curses" she screamed, her yell echoing in the white hall. Then, a dark figure appeared in front of us! It was wobbly, like a mummy. It placed its hand on my shoulder. "Aaaahhh!" We screamed. The shadow turned on the light of the lamp. It was....."Dad?" I asked. "Why are you girls screaming? You woke up mama and me." He said, turning to mommy and daddy's room. "Sorry, dada." Casity said, looking at her feet. "Now go get some rest." Dad said, his final words echoing in my head as Casity and I climbed the steps to our room. Dad followed close behind. When we got inside our beds, dad kissed us both and said "Goodnight, I love you." "Love you too daddy." Casity and I said together as one. Dad walked down the steps slowly. "I'm scared Sissy. What was that?" Casity asked in a whisper. I was glad someone was scared with me. " I'm scared too. Any anyway that was my doll Mindy." I answered. A few seconds later Casity asked, "Can I sleep with you?" "Sure, come on down." I said in relief. She climbed down and snuggled in close, against the wall and squeezed the fat frog. She sucked and chewed again. I felt hot under the cover. A few days later it was Halloween morning, a Saturday. "I'm so excited to become Casitystien." Casity bubbled. I glanced at my shabby cloak and torn stockings. Perfect for a zombie bride. I picked up my black and green lipstick and sparkly hologram fake eyelashes. My wig and bugs for my wig were perfect. I was entirely scary! Casity was really freaking me out though. In our costumes we walked outside. Kids were dressed as clowns, bats, princesses, monsters, witches, ghosts and ghouls. I spotted Emily in line for the haunted house. Casity was oozing fear.

CHAPTER 20: HALLOWEEN NIGHT

The harsh wind was the worst wind ever. It was such a burden having to hold Casity's hand that long. "Where's Casandra, mom?" I asked. I waited for her response. "I don't know she should be here by now" she answered, looking around. Adults in masks gave me chills. We caught up with Emily "Emy" I yelped. "Dane" Emily said, her arms raised, letting her long princess sleeves droop and dangle "sweet costume" she said. Just then a bright white stallion galloped on the road, stopping at Emily and my feet. Just as it stopped, the purple and gold cape on the rider, stopped. The boy's costume was all gold and purple. It was...."Nikki, nice outfit" I haven't seen you in awhile." I rubbed his velvety cape. I noticed the sparkly diamonds sewn on the bottom line. He was wearing a golden, humble crown that lay on his long wavy hair that was layered with curly locks. "What the heck are you, princy?" Casity asked, giving him an awkward look. "This is my boyfriend Nikki" I giggled. Nikki stared at me with an embarrassed smile. "Who are you, Franky?" Nikki asked politely, bowing towards her. "I'm Casity, Dana's sister." Casity oozed jerkiness.

"Oh, I didn't know you had a sister." "Yeah, Brooke and Casity, Casity is adopted." "Really?" "Yes" "Really?" "Yes, really!!" I hollered. "Here" Nikki said "take some of my candy." He gave all three of us five pieces of candy. My shoes clicked. I felt grateful. "That's very nice of you Nikki." Mom said. Casity tried the chocolate ball with the caramel inside. "Mmmm that is delicious" she said, thinking hard about it. It mushed and gushed inside her mouth and finally GULP! She swallowed. "Yummy" she giggled blushing a little. "I'm going to go catch up with my mom" Emily said with a mouth full of tootsie roll." "Ok, see ya" I said. Casity, Nikki, mom and I went from house to house getting lots of candy-o. When we reached my house again, Nikki said, "Well, I should be getting home folks." "Ok, I'll see ya then." I said, a smile breaking through my lips. I raised my arms for a hug and in return I got a ...."Mwaa kiss! Yes, I can't believe it, in front of Casity too!. "Bye prince kissy frog! Mwaa Mwaa Mwaa!" Casity said, doing imitations of Nikki. What a jerk. "Bye, man of my dreams" I said, biting my lower lip. "See ya princess!" Nikki called, riding away on his horse as wind blew my curled ends on my wig around. The cold wind nipped at my nose and toes. It felt like Jack Frost was giving me a hug. When we entered the house, I could feel warmth grab me and rub me. I smelled pumpkin pie, like the one my Grandy used to make. From behind the kitchen wall, some one was coming toward me. The footsteps were getting louder, the puffy hair showed..."Grandy!!" I screamed.

CHAPTER 21: GRANDY'S SECRET

"Rose!" Grandy screamed, licking cool whip off of her fingers. She gave me a giant hug. Yep, Grandy was making pumpkin pie! "And who do we have here? Is this Casity? I'll call you candy, like I call Dana, Rose, like her hair." Grandy giggled. And that is true, Grandy calls me Rose because it's the color of my hair. "Hello, I'm Casity, You probably knew that. Do I smell pumpkin pie? I love pumpkin pie. It's yummy. Pumpkins are delicious." Casity babbled. Oh, I understand. Casity talks fast when she is nervous! She must be scared of Grandy. Grandy is plump, short and wrinkly. She has glasses, bright blue eyes and puffy brown hair. Oh and she had looong eyelashes. Just as I was done thinking, dad came in with a plate of pumpkin pie and cool whip, setting it on a tray in front of the TV. "Mmmm, yummy." Casity hovered over the pie, licking her lips. "I know, right" I whispered into Casity's ear. It looked so gosh darn good. I watched mom cut the pieces. My piece was big and Casity's piece was just as big, Grandys piece was…well let's just say it was one up from small. We squirted whipped cream on it too! Along with a tall, warm glass of milk. "Grandy, can you please, pah.leese finally tell us the recipe of how your pie is the best with cinnamon and sugar and stuff?" I begged. Grandy tilted her head to the side, smiled without showing any teeth (only glossy pink lips), winked and went back to eating. I wonder if she will tell me her big secret. I am finally old enough to know and we have Casity here, it's perfect. After watching 'Monster House' mom took Casity into the kitchen, to wipe the green powder and makeup off of her face. Dad took the platter in. Grandys eyes followed mom, dad and Casity. Once they were gone, she jumped off the couch and grabbed my arm. Pulling me into the bathroom. "Yo, I was eating." I giggled. "Sshh" Grandy hushed furiously. We reached the bathroom, 'oh no' I thought. She quickly opened the door shoving me in. "What are you doing?" I babbled. "I'm telling you a secret" she whispered. I stared at her curiously. "Pumpkin Pie" she mouthed. Oh, now I understood, Grandy told me the secret recipe. Ooohh that sounded good, 'secret'. We exited the bathroom, Grandy holding my shoulders. She wore a suspicious grin "Grandy you'll make it obvious" I shook her hands off me and cleared my throat twice, "Sorry doll face." She said, puffing out her chin and pulling back her hands that were spread out. "What were you two doing in there?" Dad asked. No answer. "Girls, I want you to tell me what happened" "Think we can make a run for it?" Grandy whispered softly. "Let's go" I screeched. ZOOM! We were off! Dad gaped at us. He grabbed me and tickled me. "Oh oh ha ha ha heh, dad stop!" I gasped for air. "Dad! Dad!!!!" I pulled a way. After two hours of tickling, I finally fell asleep from a belly ache. Grandy went home. The next day appeared and I went to school.

CHAPTER 22: DANA FOR
STUDENT COUNCIL!!!

"Ok class, today we are doing president, vice-president, treasurer and student council elections." Mrs. Mateo announced, on that school morning in her stern voice. " I want two or four people in here to participate. Today there will be four candidates, ahem...here we go. Dennis Harrold, Dana Heartsinger, Casandra Blake and Madeline Carson." She read aloud off a piece of paper. "Yes, now I can try to make there be no basketball in gym class?" Maddie yelped. "Hey I like basketball!" Ethan Smart protested in a shout. I couldn't believe I was a candidate with Casandra. And Dennis, the class clown, and Maddie, the second popular kid in school. And finally, Kayla wasn't a candidate! "Hey Preston, say this really fast: OHWATAFOOLIAM." Ethan yelled. "Oh what a fool I am?" Preston tried. Oh brother! "Ha-ha, you're a fool!" "Nuh uh! That's not funny" "Dudes shut up, you're both fools!" Emily scowled. I glanced at Emily's skateboard T-shirt, what a tom-boy! One-hour later...ding-a-ling, lunch bell. After lunch we aligned our chairs for the school announcements. "Pupils.." Principal Tomms started. "Here it is: for President Jen and Conner for Vice President Dana Picconi and Drake, for Treasurer Elizabeth and Nate. I know right? Cool Kids! It was hard to pick! I couldn't wait this was so exciting. I could feel my chest pounding and thumping. But I knew who the Student Council kids were: "Vote Dana for student council" Emily called, handing out 'Vote for Dana' flyers. I got Emily to be my co-council. My mom bought her an orange clipboard. Michelle Pan took a flyer, Monica Cyril took a flyer, Shaylah Gardens took a flyer and Sarah Richards took a flyers. This was great! Casity made me wear lots of makeup this morning and I feel all gooey. At snack-time we handed out cookies, brownies and junk. We hung posters above water fountains and on the walls. Casandra had Hanna for a co-counselor. This was getting good. I felt frantic. Two weeks later the teachers made us vote. At the right time I stepped into the gray cubical and shut the door behind me with a clink. I grabbed the spiral pen, took a sheet of paper, and started writing. My face felt hot, but I knew who I wanted to vote for. I picked the people with the most truthful and trustful speeches. I cracked my neck as I stepped out. Oh, and yes I did write a speech, I read it to the whole class! I saw the black hair with blond streaks in a bun step in. Kayla! CLINK! I saw a 'vote for Maddie' pin on her hot purple turtleneck.

So did her posse. After the votes, Principal Tomms, went on stage and started to announce the people. "Our President is Jennifer Todds, Our Vice-President is Drake Barber, Our Treasurer is Elizabeth Coleman and student Council is …." My heart pounded, sweat gathered on my cheeks, I felt like vomiting. 'Oh no here goes' I whimpered in my head. "There appears we have 2 student council children." Principal Tomms said. "One is….Casandra Blake…." The students roared. "…and our next contestant is last but not least Madeline Carson!!" He announced.

CHAPTER 23: THE LOST BEST FRIEND

"What?" I teared up. NO! No way! This was way too unfair! Too unfair. I couldn't see through the tears that gathered in my eyes. A rock clump stuck in my throat and hurt badly. Casandra walked up to me cheerfully. "Can you believe it? I got to be Student council!" she beamed. I tried to speak and the chunky clump wiggled. "I..I'm really..Uh, um, well, yea, sure....I guess.: I coughed up. A few minutes later, Emily walked up to me and stroked my shoulder. I just stared at the tile floor for a moment thinking, what the heck just happened? "I'm sorry kiddo." She said. "It's ok it's not your fault." I said weakly. I could feel my feet sinking into the floor. Shaylah G. came up to me and said, "I voted for you Dana" that made me feel better. I forced a smile. "Yeah me too!" Sarah R. shouted, her arm clinging with Caitlyn Cotey's. "Hey, me too/" Monica Cyrus spoke up. I felt really happy. The sun showed through the broad glass windows on me like a spotlight, making me feel warm. Emily hugged me. "You didn't have to do that Em." I perked. "I know, I wanted to" she giggled. After school, I walked up to Casandra. "Hey are you still coming over to watch 'Alvin and the Chipmunks'" I asked her. That was OUR favorite show until... "Yeah, um , about that, since Maddie is getting picked up, I'm gonna watch it on her screen in her car. Turns out she likes that show too!" she said. WHAT! Just then , I noticed they were holding hands. They really must have got along at lunch and recess! How could Casandra dump our show! For Maddie? If that's the way Casandra wanted it, then that's how it will be. I avoided Casandra for seven days now and it really helped. I got new friends now. Two days later, Casandra said, "Hey, oh woops, sorry person, she had bumped into me accidentally at gym class. And she calls me a 'person'? Who does she think she is? I felt warm in my uniform sweatpants. We only have uniforms for gym, my favorite subject. I love sports and our gym teacher Ms. Applegate. She is so pretty and fun. "Person? What was all that about?" Hannah asked me. "Dunno, I think she hates me." I folded my arms across my chest. So did Hannah and she shoved her tongue up her inside tip lip. She does that when she is mad. "You mean despise, detest or loathe?" she said. "She doesn't let people say 'hate'. She says it's a bad word and her mom wont' let her say it. Casandra and Maddie were giggling. I couldn't hear it, but I could see it. We started soccer and Maddie and Casandra were chatting and laughing. Oafs! A week later, and guess what happened, Principal Tomms had big news, something that I loved something that I hated, or should I say loathed. It was the ....school dance! The nerds were looking forward to this for a looong time. I didn't know who I would take or who would take me. And it couldn't be Nikki because it has to be someone in school. I couldn't breathe. No Nikki? Then I didn't know. But I had a shot with a popular boy. I pal around with them sometimes. I guess I'm a tomboy like Emily.

CHAPTER 24: THE DANCE
WITH_____

The next school morning, at my locker I found a bouquet of bright pink flowers. I gazed at them. The card read: Be mine? I invite you to the school dance. Meet me in the Cafeteria. I'll wear a blue sweater. Love, Anonymous. At first, I thought it was a mistake, but then I knew two things. There is only one boy who knows my combination and wears sweaters all the time. My old pal Zach. I rushed to the cafeteria. Yep, I saw it, blue sweater, talking to Rob and Jacob, the cool kids. Zach was funny and sweet. We , and for we I mean, Casandra, Zach and me, we used to hang out a lot. But as we grew older, we made new friends and became kinda cool. "Yo, Zach, dude!" I yelled to him. "Sup, Dane?" he came up to me and swung an arm around my shoulders. "Got your icky flowers." I giggled. "Oh I totally messed up dude, I got you flowers instead of toenail clippings." He acted ashamed. But that made me laugh more. "Shut up " I punched his arm. Good memories! The night of the dance, I wore a long puffy, sparkly blue dress, with my hair in piggy tails and lots of blue jewelry and make up. Guess who made me wear it..Casity! Blue shiny high heels fit nicely, oh and no gloves. I wouldn't be that prissy. I entered the giant school doors and found Zack at the punch table, in the cutest tuxedo with a pink tie and orange vest inside. He was chatting with Emily and the cool kids. Zack is so close to being one. "Hey what are you doin?" I asked, curiously. "Hey, I gotcha some punch" He said quickly. Zach has soft black hair and brownish medium skin. He's Italian but does not have the accent. And his eyes are a glittery green. Emily's dress was long, skinny, silky and orange. She was out with Rob. "Wanna, um, uh…gulp…a dance?" I asked. Zach and Rob looked shocked. "Um, ok, yah, sure" Zach blushed. We walked to the center floor, I guess dance floor) and stood on the blue 'School Spirit' circle. Apparently it was supposed to light up when the spot light hit it cause the spot light beamed on us and the blue glow showed through my dress. It made the ceiling sparkly. Dummies! We stepped over. "Duh" Zach said, which meant he was doing it to himself! We danced a lot but my feet started hurting. I went out to the marble terrace. A few minutes later, a cold hand was placed on my sleeveless shoulder. I widened my eyes. "Heh! I gasped, but when I turned around I saw Casandra. "Hey sorry, I didn't mean to hurt your feelings." She said sadly. "Hey, that's ok, where's Maddie?" I asked suspiciously. "Who cares, we broke up. She called you a loser." She hugged me. "C'mon let's go dance!" She said pertly, shaking and boogying. "Ok!" I said. We danced, barefoot. I felt good that night, driving home. The moon looked gorgeous and when I left school, slow soft music was playing in the wings. I also got my B.F.F. back.

CHAPTER 25: A NEW AND OLD BEGINNING

The next day felt cold and breezy, but inside of me, I felt warm and cozy. The school flag stood high, flapping and snapping in the cold wind. Smoke puffed out of my mouth. It was frosty. Inside, the school was warm. I made up with Hannah, Emily and Casandra. Maddie was whispering something in Kayla's ear, but, I know Maddie was not a mean girl. I swished my saliva around in my mouth. A familiar voice behind me that kinda sounded like John Travolta said, "Hey Princess Dana" I turned around. "Shut your trap, Casity made me do it!" I hissed. He stopped laughing and stood there quietly staring at me. he didn't know who Casity was hahahahaha. School felt like it took forever and ever. When it was over it was just another normal day. I just layed on my bed that day and exhaled. I snuggled with Mr. Snufalupagus, my old tattered stuffed elephant. It started raining and I squirmed under the covers. Casity was just getting home from second grade. She stomped up the stairs and thrashed her book bag on the floor near the closet. Nikki called on the phone and said he just bought a giant catapult and his dad set it up in the backyard. He said I could come over and check it out. After all tomorrow was Saturday. I couldn't wait. I invited Emily, Casandra and Hannah over the next day to see the catapult too. Nikki also said we could launch some of the stuff we didn't want. He would lauch them into the dark woods and never see them again. I knew just the two things I would bring to catapult. Casity was going to catapult her broken mirror. But, I was going to launch something better. Casity, Emily, Hannah Casandra and I were driven to Nikki's house which wasn't too far away. Everyone put their future-launched things in their own plastic bags. I put mine in a suitcase so they could fit and that no one could see. We reached Nikki's house and ran with our stuff to the backyard. The catapult was huge and wooden with a cup-like ending to hold the stuff. Nikki launched a few rocks and then went Casity, Emily and Hannah. Their things whipped across the sky. Then Casandra went and pulled on the cup. WHIP! They went flying. I was up. "Here goes", I whispered to myself. I unzipped the suitcase and pulled out the two things. Everyone ooh'ed and ahh'ed. I put Mindy and Chelsea in the cup and flung them. "Curses!!" they both screeched, as they flew above the trees. They were gone! I was happy because I had my friends and boyfriend, the dolls gone, Zach back, Casity and a great life. This is the end of my story. Thank you and remember: FOLLOW YOUR DREAMS!